UNICORN ACADEMY

Olivia touched her red hair, wishing she could have a blue streak to match Snowflake's mane. Snowflake nuzzled her leg. "We'll bond soon," she said. "There's still time."

LOOK OUT FOR MORE ADVENTURES AT

UNICORN ACADEMY

Sophia and Rainbow

Scarlett and Blaze

Ava and Star

Isabel and Cloud

Layla and Dancer

Olivia and Snowflake

★ ★ ★

UNICORN ACADEMY

Olivia and Snowflake

JULIE SYKES
illustrated by LUCY TRUMAN

A STEPPING STONE BOOK™

Random House 🏠 New York

Text copyright © 2018 by Julie Sykes and Linda Chapman
Cover art and interior illustrations copyright © 2018 by Lucy Truman

Visit us on the Web! rhcbooks.com

Educators and librarians, for a variety of teaching tools, visit us at
RHTeachersLibrarians.com

Library of Congress Cataloging-in-Publication Data
Title: Olivia and Snowflake / Julie Sykes; illustrated by Lucy Truman.
Description: First American edition. | New York: Random House, [2019]
Series: Unicorn Academy; 6 | "A Stepping Stone Book." | Originally published:
London: Nosy Crow Ltd., 2018.
Summary: Olivia hopes to bond with her unicorn, Snowflake, before
graduation day, but someone has set out to ruin the graduation ball
and a secret Olivia has been keeping may be revealed.
Identifiers: LCCN 2018047507 | ISBN 978-1-9848-5169-7 (trade pbk.) |
ISBN 978-1-9848-5171-0 (lib. bdg.) | ISBN 978-1-9848-5170-3 (ebook)
Subjects: | CYAC: Unicorns—Fiction. | Magic—Fiction. | Secrets—Fiction. |
Friendship—Fiction. | Boarding schools—Fiction. | Schools—Fiction.
Classification: LCC PZ7.S98325 Oli 2019 | DDC [Fic]—dc23

Printed in the United States of America
10 9 8 7 6 5 4
First American Edition

For Jessica Broom and April Marshall

"Stay very still," Olivia whispered to Snowflake as they hid behind the marble statue of a flying unicorn.

"Should we go now?" asked Snowflake eagerly. The December air was icy, and Snowflake's breath froze in little clouds as she spoke.

"Not yet," said Olivia, her green eyes on Isabel, who was patrolling in front of the apple tree that the girls were using as base in their game of tag. "We need to wait until Isabel and Cloud get distracted." Her hand flew to her mouth. "Oh no! I think I'm going to . . . *Aaaatishooo!*"

"There they are!" yelled Isabel.

"Go, Snowflake!" shrieked Olivia. Snowflake leaped out from behind the statue, the sunlight making the silver and blue stars on her white coat shine. She charged toward the apple tree, swerving nimbly around Cloud. Olivia's red hair flew out behind her as Snowflake tried her hardest to get

to base, but Scarlett and Blaze, who were also catchers in the game, came galloping up from the right-hand side. Scarlett's arm was outstretched. Snowflake tried to get past Blaze, but Blaze was one of the fastest unicorns at Unicorn Academy, and Scarlett's hand lightly tagged Olivia's arm.

"Got you!"

Isabel whooped. "Way to go, Scarlett!"

"Sorry, Snowflake," Olivia apologized as they came to a stop.

"It doesn't matter," whinnied Snowflake, shaking her long mane. "It's fun whether we're the catchers or the people hiding!"

Isabel looked around. "Come out! Come out! Wherever you are!" she sang to their three friends, who were still hidden.

Olivia caught a glimpse of a multicolored mane behind a rosebush. "Sophia and Rainbow are over there!" she cried. "Catch them!"

The game continued until all the girls from Sapphire dorm had been caught.

"I need a rest!" said Olivia, fanning her face.

"Me too," said Layla, trotting up on Dancer.

"Play for a little longer, pleeease?" begged Scarlett. "It's our last weekend before the graduation ball. There won't be time to play next week, and then after that we'll all be going home."

The six girls from Sapphire dorm sighed. They had started at Unicorn Academy almost a year ago. In that time, they had all been given their own unicorn to love and bond with, and they'd had loads of exciting adventures together.

"It's going to be so strange not being here any longer," said Ava, looking around wistfully.

"I'll still be here," Olivia pointed out. "Snowflake hasn't discovered her magic yet, and we haven't bonded, so I won't be allowed to graduate."

Bonding was the highest form of friendship. When a person and their unicorn bonded, a

4

strand of the person's hair turned the same color as the unicorn's mane, showing they were friends for life. From that moment on, it was their duty to help protect Unicorn Island—the beautiful land where they lived. Olivia's friends all had a colorful streak in their hair—Sophia's was multicolored like Rainbow's mane, Ava's was purple, Isabel's was silver and blue, Scarlett's was red and gold, and Layla, who had bonded with Dancer most recently, had an indigo, yellow, and pink streak.

Olivia touched her own red hair, wishing she could have a blue-and-silver streak to match Snowflake's mane. As if sensing her sadness, Snowflake turned and nuzzled her leg. "We'll bond soon," she told Olivia. "There's time before graduation."

"Yes, there's still ten days!" said Sophia. "We'll help you find Snowflake's magic so we can all graduate together."

"We're not leaving you here with horrible Valentina, Delia, and Jacinta," said Scarlett. "They haven't bonded with their unicorns yet either."

Olivia felt a warm tingly feeling rush through her. Her friends were the best, and if anyone could help her, they could! "Thanks. But look, it won't be so bad if I don't graduate with all of you. My little sister, Matilda, is starting in January, so at least I'll know someone."

"You *are* going to graduate," declared Isabel. "And we are all going to meet up regularly. I know we live far away from each other, but we can sleep over at each other's houses. My room is tiny, but it's so warm in my part of the island that we can sleep outside in hammocks."

"My room's small too, but Dad lets me sleep in one of the empty greenhouses when I have a sleepover," said Ava, whose parents ran a plant nursery.

Olivia's stomach squirmed as everyone described their houses and what fun they'd have all squeezing in for sleepovers. She had a secret she still hadn't told her friends, despite knowing them for almost a year. Olivia's home was like a palace, with twelve bedrooms, an indoor swimming pool,

and a tennis court and lake. But although Olivia's parents were rich, they didn't spoil their two daughters. They believed in working hard—they both had jobs, and the girls were expected to help out at home with the cleaning.

Olivia hadn't told the others about her home and family. When she'd first met them, she hadn't wanted to mention it because she didn't want it to sound like she was showing off. Then it had somehow gotten too late to tell them, and she had ended up keeping it a secret. Whenever any of the others asked, she just changed the subject. It had seemed easier that way, but it was going to cause problems if her friends wanted to visit her house.

"What's your place like, Olivia?" asked Isabel curiously. "Where will we sleep when we come to your house?"

Olivia forced herself to laugh. "Let's see if I graduate first. Now I'm going to go back to the stables. I promised Snowflake I'd practice braiding her mane and tail with rainbow ribbons for the graduation ball, didn't I, Snowflake?"

Snowflake hid her surprise. "That's right," she agreed.

Olivia stroked Snowflake's neck, grateful she'd backed up her lie.

"I'll come with you," offered Layla. "I love braiding Dancer's mane, and you can tell me about your family. I didn't even know you had a little sister." She smiled at her. "I guess I never asked though."

Olivia's tummy twisted. In the last few months, she had become good friends with quiet, clever Layla, but she didn't want to tell her about her family. "Sorry, Layla. But do you mind if I just go back with Snowflake?"

Layla blinked. "Oh. Okay."

"I really want to spend some time with her on

9

our own. It might help us to bond," said Olivia quickly.

Layla nodded, but Olivia could see the hurt in her eyes, and she felt guilty as she rode away. She didn't say a word to Snowflake. The unicorn waited until they were on their own and then turned her head and gave Olivia a look. "What's the matter?"

"I feel horrible because I just hurt Layla's feelings, but I don't want her asking about my family. Oh, Snowflake, what am I going to do if everyone wants to come to my house next year?"

Snowflake was the only one who knew the truth about Olivia's home life. "Couldn't you just tell them about your parents? I'm sure none of them will treat you any differently."

"But they might!" said Olivia. "Look how much they laugh at Valentina." She pictured snooty Valentina from Emerald dorm. "Her family is very rich, and everyone hates her."

"That's only because Valentina is spoiled and mean," said Snowflake. "You're not like that at all. You should tell them the truth."

Olivia hesitated. Even if Snowflake was right and her friends didn't judge her, it didn't change the fact that she'd been keeping secrets from them all year. They wouldn't like that at all. No, she couldn't risk it. She couldn't bear it if they decided they didn't like her anymore.

"Let's talk about something else," she muttered.

"But—"

"No!" interrupted Olivia. "And you have to promise me you won't tell anyone."

"Of course I won't," said Snowflake, shocked. "I wouldn't do anything to make you unhappy."

To Olivia's relief she saw they had reached the stables. "Oooh, isn't it lovely and warm in here," she said, leading Snowflake inside. A cart rumbled past, filled with a bucket of sky berries. Olivia scooped up a handful and offered them to Snowflake. "I bet you're hungry after all that galloping around."

Olivia was sure Snowflake wanted to say more, but to her relief, her unicorn just sighed and ate the berries.

"I'll get some ribbons from the storeroom. I'm going to braid the prettiest rainbow ever in your mane."

Dropping a kiss on Snowflake's nose, Olivia

hurried away. It was such a relief to know her secret was safe. Snowflake was totally trustworthy and always agreed to do what Olivia wanted. If only Snowflake could find her magic and bond with her in time to graduate with the others. *But*, said a tiny voice in Olivia's head, *if Snowflake doesn't find her magic, then you won't graduate and your friends will never have to find out the truth.*

She frowned, and for the first time began to wonder if she really wanted to graduate with the others after all.

CHAPTER 2

On Monday morning the girls loaded fruit and fresh-baked pastries onto their plates. Big vases of white and pink winter lilies decorated the long tables. Scarlett pounced on Olivia and Layla as they sat down next to her. "Have you heard? Lessons are over from now on!"

"What?" said Layla.

"Yes! Billy said Ms. Primrose is about to make an announcement."

At that very moment, Ms. Primrose, their old, wise head teacher, stood and held up a hand for silence. The students stopped chattering.

"Good morning," said Ms. Primrose, her eyes twinkling in her wrinkled face. "This is a very special week, and for most of you it will be your last at Unicorn Academy. The graduation ball will take place on Friday evening. It's a tradition that each dormitory decorates one area of the academy and also puts on a show before the ball to demonstrate to the parents the skills that you and your unicorns have developed this year. Lessons are now officially over to allow you to prepare for this."

A loud cheer filled the dining hall. Hiding a smile, Ms. Primrose pulled out a piece of paper.

"Diamond dormitory, you will decorate the ballroom."

"Yay!" Billy and Jack, two of the boys from that dorm, fist-bumped each other.

"Emerald dorm . . ." Valentina de Silva and her friends looked up eagerly. "You will decorate the stables."

"The stables?" exclaimed Valentina in disgust.

"Yes, Valentina, the stables," said Ms. Primrose firmly. She raised her eyebrows, and Valentina sat back with a glare.

Ms. Primrose continued reading aloud until finally she looked at Olivia and her friends. "This year the girls in Sapphire dormitory have been extra-special guardians, stopping several attempts to sabotage Sparkle Lake and our school. Therefore, I am giving Sapphire dormitory the lake and its surroundings to decorate."

Another huge cheer almost lifted the ceiling, with the whole school clapping. *Almost the whole school,* thought Olivia, seeing Valentina give them a death stare.

As Ms. Primrose sat down, Valentina started talking angrily to her best friends, Delia and Jacinta. "I don't want to decorate the stables! My parents are trustees. I am going to demand to

16

swap. I shall see my aunt about this."

"She's not swapping with us," said Isabel firmly to the Sapphire girls. "Not after all those times we've saved the lake. Remember when someone tried to pollute it? Then a while later it froze over?"

"And there was the time it nearly flooded the school. And what about those flash flies that mysteriously appeared at the end of the summer? They killed all the leaves on the trees, which almost clogged the lake," added Scarlett.

"So many bad things have happened here this year," said Ava, tucking her chin-length dark hair behind her ears. "And not just to the lake—there was the time the sky-berry bushes all failed and the poor unicorns didn't have any berries to eat."

"I'm glad we've been able to help each time," said Layla.

Sophia looked anxious. "Who's going to look out for things here after we've left?"

"Me!" said Olivia. As she spoke, she warmed to the idea. Someone had to keep an eye on things until the person responsible for trying to sabotage the academy was caught. If she stayed, then she could help. "If I don't graduate, I'll still be here."

"But you *are* going to graduate!" protested Isabel.

"We're going to make sure of it!" chorused Sophia and Ava, linking arms with her as they left the dining hall.

On the way out, they saw Valentina talking with her aunt, Ms. Nettles, the strict Geography and Culture teacher. Ms. Nettles kept breaking off to sneeze into a tissue.

"I don't know why Valentina's so steamed up," said Ava. "The stables will be a lovely place to decorate."

"And why does Ms. Nettles keep sneezing?" said Scarlett.

"It's her hay fever," said Layla. "I bet all those vases of flowers on the tables set her off."

"I'm sorry, Valentina. There isn't anything I can do," they heard Ms. Nettles saying as they passed.

"But, Auntie——"

Ms. Nettles sneezed again. "No, Valentina. I have tried to help you this year but I cannot do anything about this. Now I really must go and get some more of my hay fever medicine, and you should concentrate on graduating." Ms. Nettles hurried off, and Valentina stomped back to Jacinta and Delia.

"I'm so glad we've got the lake to decorate!" said Isabel as Sapphire dorm went outside and breathed in the crisp air.

"Me too," agreed Olivia. The magical water of Sparkle Lake flowed up from the center of the earth and out through its fountain. From there, rivers and streams carried it around the island to keep the unicorns' magic strong, nourish the land, and help make the island a wonderful place to live.

In the wintry sunlight, rainbows glinted above

the lake and the fountain. It was beautiful but icy cold. The girls hurried inside the stables, where it was warm and cozy.

Snowflake snorted with pleasure when she saw Olivia. "I hoped you'd come. I thought you might still have to go to lessons, since we're not ready to graduate." Snowflake lowered her head. "I'm sorry I haven't found my magic yet, Olivia."

"Don't worry," said Olivia. "It's fine."

"But what will we do in the demonstration?" said Snowflake. "Everyone else will be showing off their magic."

"We can join in somehow," said Olivia, stroking her. "Maybe we can jump through hoops of fire made by Blaze, or canter across a rainbow made by Rainbow, or pick flowers that Star grows." She smiled. It sounded quite fun!

But Snowflake heaved a sigh. "I guess. I hope my parents aren't too disappointed in me, though."

"Your parents?" echoed Olivia.

"Yes, they're coming to the ball," said Snowflake.

"Oh." Olivia started to groom Snowflake's coat. She'd been so busy worrying about her own situation that she hadn't stopped to wonder how Snowflake might feel. It might be good for her if they didn't graduate, but it wasn't fair to Snowflake, particularly when her family was coming to the ball.

She sighed, feeling like she didn't know whether she wanted to graduate or not.

"Are you okay?" asked Snowflake.

"Yes, of course I am," Olivia lied.

CHAPTER 3

Later that morning, the girls headed to the gardens to work out their demonstration for the parents. They were so busy talking that, as they rounded a corner, they almost ran into Ms. Primrose and Ms. Nettles, who were standing on one of the paths. Ms. Primrose was holding a basket filled with herbs. Ms. Nettles looked angry.

"Whoops! Sorry!" gasped Scarlett as the unicorns stopped just in time.

"Girls! Whatever do you think you are doing? Please watch where you're going!" snapped Ms. Nettles. Her glasses rattled on her thin nose as she gave Blaze and Cloud a disapproving look—both unicorns had tangled manes and tails and traces of mud on their legs. "Hmm, it's looks to me like some of you in Sapphire dorm should put more effort into grooming and less into talking!"

She stalked off.

Ms. Primrose shook her head. "Don't mind Ms. Nettles, girls," she said. "She has a lot going on with the graduation ball." She reached into her basket and fed the unicorns some watermint leaves. "Here we are. A little treat for the Sapphire

unicorns." They snorted happily and munched up the leaves. "No, no more, I'm afraid, my dears," she chuckled as they looked at her hopefully. "I need the rest of these herbs for my spells."

"What spells?" asked Layla curiously.

Ms. Primrose gave a vague smile. "This and that! These are herbs for a locking spell. I'm always working to keep the academy safe, you know."

"How do you make spells, Ms. Primrose?" asked Ava. "I'd love to learn."

"It's complicated, my dear," said Ms. Primrose.

"You need to have a unicorn who is a spell-weaver like your unicorn, Sage, don't you, Ms. Primrose?" said Layla. "I've read about it. A spell-weaver puts the magic in that makes a spell work—and if you've got a spell-weaver for a unicorn, you can make spells that do all sorts of things."

"Goodness, Layla, you're very good at finding

things out, aren't you?" Ms. Primrose smiled, but Olivia noticed an unusually sharp note to her voice. "That is quite correct. Now, girls, are you happy you've been given the lake to decorate?"

The others nodded, but something about Ms. Primrose's behavior was striking Olivia as odd. What was it? Before she could figure it out, Ms. Primrose said goodbye to them. "I must be off. Have fun practicing for the demonstration, girls."

"We will!" they chorused as their kind head teacher hurried away.

★

Isabel had already thought out a plan for their demonstration. "We'll all canter in together and then stop in the center, apart from Dancer, who can fly up into the air and turn a loop-the-loop. That will be a really impressive opening! Then Blaze can create a circle of fire, Cloud can make rain to put the fire out, Star can make flowers grow where the fire was, and Rainbow can magic up a rainbow over them!"

They started to practice. A lot of the time was spent going through the difficult magical moves, and there wasn't much for Olivia and Snowflake to do.

"Should we stop now, Isabel?" called Ava after a while. "We can practice more later, but if we do too much magic our unicorns will get tired." Doing magic used up a lot of energy for the unicorns.

Isabel looked as if she was going to argue, but Layla spoke before she could. "Good plan," she said, glancing over at Olivia and Snowflake, who were standing on their own. "Why don't we give the unicorns a rest and go and do something we can all be involved with, like decorating the lake?"

Olivia gave her a grateful look. It wasn't much fun just watching.

They headed back to the stables first to let the unicorns have some sky berries. As they rode up to the door, there was a loud shriek. Olivia and the others hurried inside. The students from Emerald dorm were there, most of them looking very excited because Cupcake, Delia's unicorn, had just discovered he had finding magic that allowed him to find things that were lost. And Delia's chestnut-colored hair now had a streak of strawberry pink, the same shade as Cupcake's mane and tail.

Valentina was a little ways off from the others, her mouth pursed as if she had just sucked on a lemon. "Finding magic is so uncool!" she declared. "Seriously—I wouldn't be pleased if Golden Briar had magic like that. It's really not very impressive, is it?"

"At least Delia has bonded with Cupcake, and now they'll be able to graduate!" retorted Scarlett.

Valentina glared. "Emerald dormitory are the only students allowed in the stables while we're decorating it. If you don't go right now, I'll tell my aunt."

"Okay. Don't have a cow." Scarlett grinned. "We just wanted to get some sky berries." She grabbed a bucketful of the berries. "Come on, everyone, we've got far more important things to do."

"Yes, like decorating the lake!" said Isabel. She smiled at Delia. "Well done for finding out Cupcake's magic," she called. "I think it's cool."

"Thanks," said Delia, pleased.

"Gah!" exclaimed Valentina angrily as they left.

CHAPTER 4

Over the next few days, a constant buzz hummed through the buildings and grounds of the academy as the students and their unicorns rushed from one task to the next. Sapphire dorm made hundreds of foil stars and glittery rainbows to string around the lake. Olivia's fingers ached from cutting and gluing, and her brain ached from worry. It would be so much fun if she could graduate with her friends, but she was also desperate for them not to discover her secret.

By Wednesday afternoon, tempers were beginning to fray. Things came to a head when

Olivia, Snowflake, and their friends returned to the stables after a long session in the sand school. Valentina was there, standing on one of the automated carts, attempting to hang a model of a golden unicorn from a hook on the wall.

"Go away," she said.

"We won't disturb you," said Ava. "But we need to give our unicorns a drink."

Valentina's face turned as red as a squashed tomato. "Did you not hear? Go away. Move on— and fast!"

"Valentina, no!" squeaked Jacinta, but it was too late. The remote-controlled carts were also voice activated. The moment the words were out, the cart took off.

"Stop!" yelped Valentina. The cart stopped suddenly, sending her flying across the stables. She landed in a pile of hay with her feet in the air and the model on her head. It broke in two, raining gold beads and glitter down on her.

"That's your fault," she screamed, pointing at Ava.

"Valentina, calm down." Jacinta rushed over to help. "It wasn't Ava's fault, and there's still time to fix it."

Valentina was too angry to listen. She jumped to her feet and stomped over to Ava.

CRACK!

The noise made everyone jump.

"Tiddlywink!" Jacinta stared in wonder at her unicorn as blue sparkles, the color of a midsummer sky, floated up from her hooves. The sparkles wafted through the stables, leaving everyone they touched with a sparkly blue outline. Olivia suddenly felt as light as air. All her troubles floated away, and happiness bubbled up inside her.

Valentina smiled a huge sweet smile as she ran a hand through her hair. "Look, everyone!"

she cooed. "The gold beads from the model are making my hair sparkle. It's so pretty."

Jacinta stared at Tiddlywink with huge eyes. "You've got soothing magic!"

"Just like my mother," said Tiddlywink, looking delighted. "I can hardly believe it. Soothing magic calms tempers and turns sad occasions into happy ones."

Jacinta hugged her. When they pulled apart, everyone saw that Jacinta's brown hair had a vibrant strand of green, yellow, and orange.

"You've bonded," squealed Delia. "You're going to graduate too!"

"Oh, Jacinta, that's wonderful!" said Valentina, hugging her friend.

"Do you think we could make Tiddlywink use her magic on Valentina every day?" Ava whispered to Olivia.

Olivia grinned.

Unfortunately, by dinnertime Valentina was back to her normal self. She sat in angry silence as Jacinta and Delia compared the moment their unicorns had discovered their magic. Finally, she slammed down her knife and fork. "Will you please be quiet? Honestly! Finding magic and soothing magic? They're both rubbish! Golden Briar will have much more powerful magic than either of your unicorns. That's why it's taking longer for him to discover it."

"I'm sure you're right, Valentina," said Jacinta. "We could help you if you want, especially as it's almost graduation day."

"Oh, for goodness' sake!" Valentina stood up so fast her chair toppled over with a bang. "I don't need your help! It won't matter if Golden Briar has found his magic or not. I'll graduate anyway. My parents will see to it. They're—"

"*Trustees!*" shouted everyone in earshot.

"I hate you all!" Sticking her nose in the air, Valentina stomped out of the room.

Isabel watched her go. "I am *so* glad we don't have a Valentina in our dorm."

"I don't know." Scarlett's eyes twinkled. "Imagine the fun we could have teasing someone as stuck up and snobby as that!"

Olivia crumbled her roll and avoided meeting their eyes. Glancing across the room, she saw Ms. Primrose watching her. A hot blush flooded Olivia's cheeks. Maybe Ms. Primrose thought Olivia wanted special treatment like Valentina because she hadn't bonded with Snowflake yet either. *No*, thought Olivia. She would never try to use her parents' influence to get her own way at Unicorn Academy.

She glanced at the teachers' table again. To her alarm, Ms. Primrose was still staring at her with a strange, thoughtful look in her eyes.

CHAPTER 5

That night, Olivia lay in bed with her worries rolling around in her head. But at last, she slept. When she woke, something was tickling her nose. Olivia batted her hand in front of her face and heard a giggle.

"Olivia, wake up."

The bedroom was in darkness, but Olivia could just make out the others standing by her bed. She sat up immediately. "What's wrong?"

"Nothing," said Isabel, handing Olivia her fleece hoodie. "Put this on. We've decided we're going to help Snowflake find her magic!"

"How?" asked Olivia uncertainly.

"We've been thinking about the exact moment our unicorns got their magic. It's always happened when someone's been in danger," said Scarlett. "We thought if we could create a few *situations*, it might help Snowflake to find her magic."

"Great," croaked Olivia, wishing she really meant it.

They fetched their unicorns and headed to the gardens. It was still dark, and Sophia rode at the front, Rainbow using his magic to light the way.

Olivia stayed at the back with Layla. Olivia's thoughts were racing, and she only half listened to Layla, who, most unusually, was chattering nonstop.

"Where is everyone?" asked Olivia, suddenly realizing that Dancer had been walking so slowly, they had gotten left behind.

"I don't know," said Layla innocently.

Olivia heard an eerie rustling ahead.

"What's that?" Snowflake's white ears twitched.

Olivia gasped as spiky bushes suddenly sprang up in front of them.

"Time to get out of here." Dancer spun around and took off, sandy soil spraying up from his hooves as he galloped away. Snowflake followed, neck arched, her silver-and-blue tail streaming behind her.

"What's going on?" demanded Olivia. "What's—" She broke off as another wall of bushes shot up from the ground.

"Jump, Snowflake!" urged Dancer. Huge indigo-and-yellow wings burst from his shoulders as he flew effortlessly over the bushes. Olivia felt Snowflake's muscles bunch as if she was about to go after Dancer. She clung on tightly. Was Snowflake about to discover her magic in time to help her? Olivia was torn between relief and despair. *I don't want her to,* she thought.

"Olivia?" Snowflake faltered. "What's wrong?"

"Nothing, I'm fine."

Snowflake's hesitation cost her. Now she was too close to jump the bushes. She stopped suddenly then reared up, slashing at the bushes with her hooves.

"It's too big! I can't clear it."

CRACK!

The bushes exploded in a ball of fire that burned with bright-orange flames.

"Snowflake, move back!" shrieked Olivia.

Snowflake spun around. There was a flash of light, and a rainbow appeared, one end anchored in the sandy earth, arching over the fire. Relief rushed through Olivia. Sophia and Rainbow were saving them!

Olivia urged Snowflake on, and they galloped up the shimmering rainbow. But when they reached the top, it suddenly collapsed.

Olivia screamed and Snowflake whinnied as they plummeted earthward. But what was that? Olivia heard the roar of water, then a blue wave curled ahead of them, catching her and Snowflake on its crest. As the wave peaked, Snowflake slid down it and landed safely back on the ground. The wave disappeared, along with the giant bushes and the fire. In their place were her friends, their outlines glowing in the rising sun.

"Nothing?" said Isabel, her voice loaded with disappointment. "Not even a tiny hint of magic?"

Olivia shook her head, her heart pounding. "Not a thing. Sorry." She gulped. "That was pretty frightening though!"

"Sorry," said Ava. "We just wanted to try to help."

"I know. Thanks—I think," said Olivia, forcing a smile.

★

Back at the stables, the girls found Ms. Primrose standing beside Golden Briar's stable with Sage, her unicorn. Another unicorn—one with pink and gray swirls—was parading up and down in front of them. Ms. Primrose was nodding approvingly.

Olivia gave a strangled squeak as the unicorn turned toward them. It was Owl, the unicorn who belonged to Ms. Tring, her tutor back at home!

Was Ms. Tring here too? Were her friends about to find out her secret?

Ms. Primrose swung around. "Girls! You're up early! Well, what do you think of Sage's magic?"

The other girls exchanged puzzled looks, while Olivia continued staring at Owl, who seemed to have a faint golden glow around him. What was he doing here?

"What magic?" asked Isabel.

Ms. Primrose chuckled. "Sage and I are trying out a disguise spell."

Sage stamped his hoof. The unicorn with pink and gray swirls began to change color and size until . . .

"Golden Briar!" Everyone stared in amazement.

Golden Briar shook his head in confusion. Gathering himself together, he said, "Don't you know that it's rude to stare?" Then he stomped into his stable.

"Disguises—as I say, you never know when you might need one!" said Ms. Primrose with a wink at Sage. He banged a hoof on the ground, and a glittering cloud of multicolored sparkles fell over him. When the magical glitter faded, Golden Briar stood in his place.

"Don't you know that it's rude to stare?" the unicorn said, with a dramatic toss of his mane.

The girls burst out laughing. Olivia joined in. Of course the pink-and-gray unicorn hadn't been Owl! There was a strong similarity though. What a strange coincidence that Ms. Primrose had created a unicorn that looked just like him. A feeling of unease ran down her spine.

"Sage, is that really you?" Sophia giggled. Sage stamped his hoof again.

Pop! Golden Briar was Sage once more, laughing along with everyone.

"Sage's magic is rather clever, isn't it, dears?" laughed Ms. Primrose. "Now, come along, get those unicorns back into their stables, and run along inside. You don't want to miss your breakfast, do you?"

It really must have been just a coincidence, Olivia decided, looking at Ms. Primrose's kind face.

As she put Snowflake in her stable she said, "I'll come back after breakfast and braid your mane."

To her surprise, Snowflake shook her head. "I don't feel like having my mane braided today."

"Oh, okay," said Olivia. "We can go for a ride instead."

Snowflake looked awkward. "Actually, I think I might just have a little rest this morning instead. I'll see you this afternoon."

"All right," said Olivia. She walked away, feeling hurt. Why didn't Snowflake want to be with her? As she reached the stable entrance Snowflake whinnied, "I love you, Olivia."

"I love you too," said Olivia slowly, and she headed inside for breakfast.

CHAPTER 6

That afternoon Sapphire dorm heard shouts coming from the lake. They cantered over. Valentina and Golden Briar were standing on the grassy banks of the lake with Delia and Jacinta. A strong breeze was swirling around, making the decorations that Sapphire dorm had hung in the trees—the lanterns, the strings of glittery stars and rainbows, the banners and the streamers—all toss about and twirl wildly.

"Wind magic!" Valentina was shrieking. "Golden Briar has wind magic! Look!"

Jacinta and Delia cheered.

"Golden Briar might have found his magic," Layla whispered to Olivia, "but they still haven't bonded!"

Layla was right. There was no streak of gold in Valentina's hair.

"Watch this!" commanded Valentina. "Make a stronger wind, Golden Briar. I know—make a dust devil!"

Golden Briar hesitated. "I'm not sure I should. I've only just found my magic."

Valentina poked Golden Briar. "Do it!"

"It's not a good idea, Valentina!" called out Scarlett. "When your unicorn first discovers

49

magic, it can easily get out of control. Like Blaze's did."

"I'm not you, and Golden Briar isn't Blaze. We can do this easy-peasy!" declared Valentina. "Come on, Golden Briar. Do as I say!"

Looking anxious, Golden Briar stamped his hoof three times. A miniature tornado swirled up from the ground, churning up fallen leaves and dust. It moved across the banks of the lake toward the trees, spinning quickly.

"See!" Valentina oozed smugness. "Faster, Golden Briar. Make it go higher!"

Golden Briar stamped harder, and the dust devil doubled, then tripled in size. The leaves blurred as they spun.

"Be careful, Valentina!" cried Olivia in alarm.

"Slow it down!" said Valentina.

"I can't!" whinnied Golden Briar.

The whirlwind slammed into a tree, ripping it

up by the roots and twirling it around. Everyone started to shout and yell at Golden Briar to stop.

But Golden Briar was powerless. He pounded his hoof on the ground, but the dust devil seemed to have a life of its own. It ripped through a line of trees, uprooting them and wrecking all the decorations.

"What are we going to do?" cried Sophia.

"We need rain," said Layla. "That will stop it."

"I can help!" whinnied Cloud.

Isabel and Cloud galloped toward the whirling funnel of wind. Isabel's curly hair was blown back, and she had to cling tightly to Cloud's neck to stop herself from being swept off his back.

Snowflake pawed the ground as another tree was swept into the air and a flying branch narrowly missed Cloud. "What if they get hurt?" she said.

For a moment, Olivia was sure she saw a gold spark fly up, and she caught a whiff of burnt sugar.

Just for a second the dust devil almost seemed to freeze. The other unicorns looked around sharply at Snowflake, but then Cloud reached the whirlwind. He stamped both front feet down on the ground. Blue sparks flew up into the air above him and Isabel, and rain clouds formed right over the dust devil. It wobbled and teetered as it was bombarded with fat raindrops.

"It's shrinking," whooped Sophia as the dust devil collapsed like a deflating balloon, first to a brisk wind, then a breeze, until the air finally stilled. There was a long moment of silence as everyone looked around at the ripped-up trees, the leaves everywhere, and the broken branches tangled up with smashed decorations.

Olivia's eyes filled with tears as she remembered the hours she and the others had spent making those decorations, but she blinked them back. At least no one had been hurt.

Isabel galloped furiously over to Valentina. "Valentina! That's why you don't show off with magic! Look what you've done. You've wrecked the trees *and* our decorations."

Valentina shrugged. "Oh, don't overreact. My aunt's unicorn, Thyme, can regrow the trees, and as for the decorations, well, they're hardly worth making a song and dance about, are they? You can make some more." She jumped onto Golden Briar and rode away.

Jacinta and Delia shot Sapphire dorm apologetic looks and followed her.

"I can't believe Valentina!" exploded Ava. "She didn't even say thank you to Isabel and Cloud!"

"And our decorations are totally ruined!" said Sophia.

"I'm just glad no one got hurt," said Olivia, hugging Snowflake as Isabel and Cloud cantered back. "You were amazing!" she called.

"Absolutely brilliant!" said Scarlett, high-fiving Isabel. "If it hadn't been for Cloud's magic, who knows what would have happened."

"Someone else's magic might have been able to help," said Blaze, shooting a look at Snowflake.

"Yes, Snowflake, try stamping your hoof again—harder this time," Star joined in.

"Why?" asked Olivia. "What's going on?"

"Didn't you see?" Star looked at Olivia, her dark eyes bright with hope. "Snowflake almost got her magic back then. Just before Cloud made it rain. Something happened."

"I definitely smelled magic over here," put in Rainbow.

"That's the second time today," whickered Dancer. "I really think you're almost there, Snowflake. Go on, try!"

Snowflake lifted her hoof and stamped it on the ground. They all waited expectantly but nothing happened. Snowflake heaved a sigh of disappointment. "Sorry," she said. "You must have all imagined it. Come on, let's go back to the stables and find Thyme so he and Star can regrow the trees."

They started heading back. Olivia was frowning. What was it Dancer had said?

"Snowflake," she said, leaving a little gap between her and the others. "What did Dancer mean when he said *that's the second time today*?"

There was a long silence, then Snowflake said awkwardly, "I didn't want to keep it a secret, but I didn't tell you in case it made you feel bad. My unicorn friends offered to help me find my magic this morning. That's why I didn't want my mane braided. We went to the meadows to practice magic instead. You don't mind, do you?"

"No . . . of course not." Olivia was lost for words. Snowflake said she was her best friend, so why hadn't she been honest with her?

"It didn't work anyway," said Snowflake sadly. "I guess we're really not going to graduate."

"I guess not," whispered Olivia, feeling all tangled up inside.

CHAPTER 7

Dressed in pajamas with a hoodie on top, Olivia crept downstairs and went outside. The rainbow-colored lake glimmered in the moonlight, and the frosty air pinched her cheeks. Olivia hopped from the shadow of the buildings, tiptoeing across the grass until she reached the stables. It was warm and welcoming, with the soft snuffles of the sleeping unicorns. Olivia continued along to Snowflake's stall.

"Olivia, can't you sleep either?" Snowflake stumbled to her hooves. There was an awkward silence.

"I'm sorry." Olivia and Snowflake spoke together.

"You first, Snowflake."

"No, you."

Olivia took a deep breath. "Look, I really am sorry. We should be able to trust each other and tell each other the truth. I don't want to have secrets between us."

Snowflake hung her head, not meeting Olivia's eye. "I'm sorry too. I didn't mean to hurt you, but I *really* want to graduate. My parents will be so disappointed if I have to stay here for another year. This last week it's felt like . . ." Snowflake shook her head. "Forget it. Can you forgive me, Olivia? I promise to tell you everything from now on."

"It's felt like what?"

A rosy flush spread up Snowflake's neck. "You'll think I'm being silly, but sometimes it feels like you

59

don't want me to find my magic. It's ridiculous, I know!"

Now it was Olivia's turn to go red. "It's not! I really want to help you find your magic and for us to bond and everything. But . . ." She took a deep breath. Trust worked two ways. Snowflake had been honest with her, and now she had to be honest back. "Sometimes, I can't help thinking that it might be easier to stay at the academy for another year. Then no one would find out about my parents. You know how much Isabel and Scarlett hate Valentina for acting like she's better than other people."

"But you're not Valentina—you don't act like that," said Snowflake. "You have to trust your friends, Olivia."

Olivia played with a strand of Snowflake's long mane. "You're right," she said at last. "If I'm honest with my friends and they don't like me, then they're not really very good friends, I guess."

"No more secrets, then?" said Snowflake hopefully.

"None!" Olivia flung herself at Snowflake and hugged her tightly. "I promise to tell you and my friends everything from now on."

Olivia was so happy she felt she might explode as she and Snowflake cuddled up together in the straw and talked until they finally fell asleep. It didn't matter if she couldn't graduate. At least she could be honest with her friends. She just hoped they would still like her after she told them the truth.

★

"Olivia! What are you doing here?"

Olivia woke to see Layla peering at her. Where was she? Realizing she was next to Snowflake, she remembered. "I don't know. I guess I just fell asleep."

"You'd better get up. We've got loads to do before the parents arrive this evening for the ball. Oh my goodness!" Layla's mouth hung open. "Look at your hair. When did you and Snowflake bond?"

Olivia tipped her head forward and stared at the blue-and-silver streak brightening her red hair. "Look, Snowflake," she gasped as Snowflake sleepily opened her eyes. "We've finally bonded!"

Hope flickered across Snowflake's face.

"Hooray! If only we could find my magic, then maybe we can graduate too."

"There's still time today." Olivia hugged her. "You know, it might happen now that there are no secrets between us. That might have been what was holding you back."

"Secrets?" echoed Layla.

"Yes, I've got to tell you something—" Olivia broke off as Valentina arrived, striding through the stable with Jacinta and Delia scurrying behind.

"Get busy grooming Golden Briar, you two. I want him to look his best for my meeting with Mommy, Daddy, and Ms. Primrose. They're going to persuade Ms. Primrose to let me graduate."

Olivia rolled her eyes at Layla. She couldn't tell her now with Valentina there. Anyway, maybe it would be better to confess her secret to all her friends together. "Let's go and get breakfast," she said with a grin.

Olivia waited until all her friends were sitting down at the breakfast table. "Listen up, everyone. There's something I need to—"

"Olivia?"

"Yes." Olivia glanced up at Sam, from Amber dorm.

"Ms. Nettles wants all students not graduating to meet her in the Tropical Garden. She'll be waiting on the rope bridge over the river."

"Thanks, I'll go in a minute." Now that Olivia had decided to be honest with her friends, she wanted it over and done with.

"Ms. Nettles said *immediately*, and you know how upset she gets when she's kept waiting."

Olivia sighed. "Thanks, Sam. Guess I'd better go, then. See you later, everyone."

"Hurry back," said Scarlett. "You still have

time to find Snowflake's magic. It might be easier now that you've bonded."

"I'll try." Olivia hurried outside and strode through the academy grounds. It was a long walk to the Tropical Garden. The farther she got from the main building, the quieter it became. It was strange that there wasn't anyone else around, not even Valentina. Maybe Valentina's parents had arrived and persuaded Ms. Primrose to allow her to graduate anyway.

A bamboo fence marked the entrance to the Tropical Garden. Olivia blinked as she went inside. Tall trees with matted trunks, some covered with thick green ivy, towered above her. The chatter and screech of birds was deafening. Wishing she had waited for someone else to walk with, Olivia hurried on until she heard the rush of water. *Thank goodness*. She came upon the rope bridge suddenly and was surprised by how narrow it was. What a strange place for Ms. Nettles to pick for a gathering.

Olivia had just reached the middle of the bridge, holding on to the thick rope handles, when she heard a footstep behind her. Relieved, she turned, but something dropped over her head. Olivia squeaked as her arms were pinned to her sides.

Her heart pounded, and she fought bravely inside the musty sack, but her attacker was strong.

"Stop struggling and come with me!" hissed a voice. "Be good and I'll return you to your parents safe and sound." It was a woman's voice, and it sounded familiar. But before Olivia could figure out who it was, she felt a hand on her head and heard a spell being muttered, and then everything went black and she knew no more.

CHAPTER 8

When Olivia woke up, she found she was in a thatched hut with straw on the floor and a boarded-up window. Her head felt fuzzy as she scrambled to her feet.

The words her attacker had spoken came back to her. "Be good and I'll return you to your parents safe and sound." Olivia groaned. Her parents had often warned her that someone might try to kidnap her in order to get a ransom from them—a large sum of money in exchange for her release. But they'd told her she would be absolutely safe at Unicorn Academy. Ms. Primrose

and all the other teachers would protect her.

Olivia banged on the door. "Let me out!" Anger and fear gave her extra strength, but no matter how hard she hit the door, it wouldn't open. Exhausted, she finally gave up. Who had kidnapped her? She thought back to what had happened. Was it Ms. Nettles who had put the sack over her head and brought her here? She remembered how someone had touched her head and said words that had made her pass out. It hadn't sounded like Ms. Nettles's sharp, high voice at all. But if it wasn't Ms. Nettles, who was it?

She shook her head. Right now, the important thing was getting out of here. She tried to pry the wooden board away from the window, but although she worked until her fingers were sore, it wouldn't budge.

She thought about Snowflake. Surely her

unicorn would realize there was something wrong when she didn't turn up to get her ready for graduation. They'd bonded and promised to have no more secrets. Snowflake would know that she would never just disappear without telling her what she was doing.

Olivia sank to the floor. *Oh, Snowflake,* she thought. *Please come.*

Olivia had nearly given up hope of a rescue when she heard the clatter of unicorn hooves accompanied by the sound of voices. She rushed to the door and banged on it.

"Help! Help!" she shouted.

"Olivia, is that you?" Someone rattled the door handle.

Relief made Olivia dizzy as she recognized Scarlett's familiar voice. "Yes! Someone trapped me in here!"

"Don't worry," called Scarlett. "We'll soon have you out. It's locked, but Blaze can burn a hole in the wood. Stand back so she doesn't burn you by mistake."

Olivia stood well away from the door. There was a muffled crack and a flash followed by the smell of burning wood. Red-gold flames crackled through the door, burning a hole. Olivia worried the whole shed might catch on fire, but when the

hole was large enough for her to climb through, the flames died down.

Helped by several hands, Olivia ducked out through the hole. She blinked and took a deep breath of fresh air. Snowflake was instantly at her side, pushing her muzzle in Olivia's hair and whickering softly. Olivia flung her arms around her. She'd never been so pleased to see her in all her life.

"Oh, Olivia, I'm so glad you're okay," whickered Snowflake. "When you didn't come to the stables to get me ready, I knew something bad had happened. I just knew it."

Layla continued the story. "We asked Ms. Nettles where you were. She said that all students not graduating were in the library with Ms. Rosemary. But when we looked, you weren't there, and no one had seen you. That's when we knew something was wrong."

"Rainbow used his magic that lets him see things that are far away, and we saw you in this shed," said Sophia.

"What happened?" demanded Isabel.

"Wait, let's not talk here," said Layla quickly. "Whoever locked Olivia in might come back at any time."

They headed through the Tropical Garden until they found a quiet mango grove, and then Olivia told them everything.

"But why would someone want to kidnap you, Olivia?" said Ava.

Olivia felt herself start to tremble. Her moment had finally arrived. "Well," she said slowly. "There is a reason. I know I should have told you sooner, but I was scared you wouldn't be my friends anymore. I'm not exactly who you think I am. . . ."

When Olivia finished explaining, everyone stared at her.

"You thought you couldn't tell us this because we wouldn't like you?" said Isabel.

"That we'd think you were like Valentina?" said Ava, her eyes wide.

Olivia swallowed. "Yes."

"But you're nothing like Valentina!" burst out Sophia.

"Nothing at all!" agreed Scarlett. "We don't like her because she's snobby and rude. We really like you, and it doesn't matter how much money your family has."

Olivia could have cried with relief. "Really?"

"Yes!" they all chorused.

"So that's why you were kidnapped?" said Layla. "So that your parents would pay a ransom?"

Olivia nodded. "I think so."

"But who kidnapped you?" said Ava.

"I don't know. I was told Ms. Nettles wanted to meet with me, but the person who grabbed me

didn't sound anything like Ms. Nettles. I think I was just starting to recognize the voice when she said a spell and I blacked out."

"A spell?" Layla's eyes widened. "Ms. Primrose does magic with spells. Was it her?"

The others erupted.

"Ms. Primrose!"

"Layla, that's nuts!"

"Ms. Primrose wouldn't kidnap Olivia!"

"Wait!" Olivia held up her hands. "Maybe it's not that shocking an idea." She'd been thinking things through while she'd been in the shed. "When Ms. Primrose disguised Golden Briar this morning, he looked just like my tutor's unicorn, Owl. What if she'd been planning on using a unicorn disguised as Owl to lure me away?"

"But it can't be Ms. Primrose," said Isabel shaking her head. "Why would she kidnap you?"

Olivia frowned. She didn't really have an

answer to that. Why would their head teacher want to kidnap her? "I don't know," she admitted.

Sophia shook her head. "I think it's much more likely to be Ms. Nettles. In fact, I bet she's the person who's been causing trouble all along. When Ava and I went looking for sky-berry bushes, we were attacked by someone on a unicorn doing plant magic, and Thyme, Ms. Nettles's unicorn, has plant magic!"

"Ms. Nettles was seen by Sparkle Lake with a little potion bottle just before it froze over," added Scarlett. "And, Olivia, you saw her by the trees drinking from a potion bottle just before the flash flies arrived."

"And when the flash flies invaded the trees by the lake, she knew that fire beetles could help get rid of them, but she didn't go and find any and she forbade Layla from going," said Isabel triumphantly. "She's so mean too. It's got to be her!"

"No! I think you're all wrong!" Blood rushed to Layla's cheeks as all eyes fell on her.

Olivia gave Layla's hand a quick encouraging squeeze. She knew how much Layla hated speaking out in front of everyone, but whatever Layla wanted to say, she wanted to hear it. Layla might be the quietest of them all, but she was also the cleverest.

"I've talked to Ms. Nettles," said Layla, "and she really cares about the island and loves everything in it, from beetles to unicorns. She isn't always mean. She was very kind to me when I was scared of galloping Dancer. She told me she hates galloping too." Layla's eyes widened. "Of course! Don't you see? She can't have been the person chasing Sophia and Ava down the mountain. They were going at a flat-out gallop, and Ms. Nettles doesn't like galloping. I'm sure she's not the person who is sabotaging the school.

When I got back with the fire beetles, she seemed really delighted. It was Ms. Primrose who tried to stop me putting them into the trees. You know, I think it's Ms. Primrose, not Ms. Nettles!"

The sound of a slow handclap broke the silence. They all jumped and swung around. Ms. Primrose was sitting astride Sage behind them. Her blue eyes glittered like ice. "Well, well, well. I always suspected you were the one I needed to watch out for, Layla. You really are a very clever girl. I had everyone else fooled, didn't I?"

The girls were too shocked to say a word.

Ms. Primrose chuckled at their expressions, but there was no warmth in her laugh. "Layla is correct. I *am* the one who has been sabotaging the school. And yes, I did kidnap Olivia. A large ransom from her family would have been very useful for my master plan, but now Valentina's parents have provided me with the money I need

in exchange for allowing Valentina to graduate."

"What master plan?" said Isabel.

"Do you think I want to be a head teacher forever?" sneered Ms. Primrose. "For too long I have followed the rules. Now it's my turn to have power! By weakening the unicorns, I can pave the way for my partner to take control of Unicorn Island! And with our combined magic, we shall rule the land together."

Olivia and her friends gasped. What evil person was Ms. Primrose working with?

"No," said Layla in horror. "We'll tell everyone what you're planning!"

Ms. Primrose laughed. "Oh no, you won't, my dear. I'm afraid this is where your interference ends!"

She tossed a handful of herbs into the air and called out a spell. A bolt of magic fired at Dancer's hooves. He jumped back just in time as

the forest floor around him exploded with leaves and branches. Another bolt followed and then another. The unicorns leaped around, trying to avoid the missiles.

Ms. Primrose's laughter rose to a shriek.

Star tried to help by making ivy to sweep Sage off his feet, but Ms. Primrose blasted it to smithereens. "You can't stop me!" she cried.

"Quick! Get out of here, everyone!" yelled Isabel. They turned and galloped out of the mango grove, with bolts of dark magic exploding around them and Ms. Primrose's cackles filling the air.

CHAPTER 9

Branches and vines snatched at Olivia's clothes and hair, almost dragging her from Snowflake as they pounded through the Tropical Garden. The air rang with the sound of magical explosions. Olivia urged Snowflake on. When she saw the bamboo gate ahead, her heart skipped. Surely Ms. Primrose would stop chasing them once they were out in the open!

BANG! In a flash of crimson, the gate exploded, throwing poles of bamboo into the air like javelins. The remains came crashing down in a pile, blocking the way out.

"Stand back!" Sophia and Rainbow pulled up beside them. Rainbow stamped his hoof, filling the air with glittery magic. A rainbow sprang from his hoof, arching over the fallen gate.

Cloud and Dancer galloped over the rainbow bridge, followed by Star, Blaze, Snowflake, and Rainbow. As Rainbow's hooves touched the ground, the bridge dissolved. Ms. Primrose's screech of fury rang in Olivia's ears as she and

her friends continued
across the grasslands
toward the lake. Ms. Primrose
was some way behind. It was almost as
though she was letting them escape—but why?

"To Sparkle Lake!" cried Isabel. "We have to
protect it!"

The unicorns increased their speed. There
was no one else anywhere to be seen—they were
all inside getting ready for the ball. Reaching
the banks of the lake, they turned to see

Ms. Primrose and Sage directly behind them.

"Got you!" crowed Ms. Primrose. The loudest clap of magic yet thundered around them. Six bolts of magic arched overhead, burning with a trail of fire and landing in a perfect ring around the lake and the girls. An explosion followed, lighting up the lake with an orange glow as the surrounding trees caught fire. Thick smoke billowed into the air.

"We're trapped!" gasped Olivia.

The trees crackled and spat as the fire gobbled them up. Flames leaped from the burning branches, running across Sparkle Lake to the fountain, which ignited in a rainbow of color.

Blaze stamped her hoof and attempted to control the flames, but the magic fire was too strong for her to put out. "I can't do anything," she cried.

Cloud made a rain cloud, but as the droplets

fell they just sizzled away and the flames burned on fiercely.

"What do we do now?" squeaked Sophia. "Rainbow's too exhausted to make another rainbow bridge."

"Dancer and I could fly and get help, but it would mean leaving you all behind," said Layla.

"Go!" urged Sophia. "Get help!"

Dancer spread his wings, but before he could take off, a section of the circle of fire extinguished for a moment and Ms. Primrose came cantering through on Sage, firing another spell straight at them as she did so. Before any of them could move, a blazing thorny cage grew up around them all. Ms. Primrose's eyes were wild as she circled them.

"There'll be no more meddling from Sapphire dorm now!" she spat. "There is nothing you can do to stop me! This time you're too late to save the

lake. I've put a spell on the locks of the school so the teachers and students are stuck inside. The lake will burn, the school will shut down, and the unicorns will be so weakened that with a few powerful spells my partner and I can take over!"

Ms. Primrose sent more magic spinning at the bushes and trees. The flames grew higher and hotter around the girls.

"One last shot!" she shouted, raising her hands. "One final direct hit and then it is all over for you!"

"No!" whinnied Snowflake, stamping her front hooves in anger. Olivia saw a gold spark fly up and smelled the familiar smell of burnt sugar. "I won't let you hurt everyone!"

"How will you stop me?" laughed Ms. Primrose. "You haven't even found your magic."

Olivia gasped. "Stamp again, Snowflake!"

As Snowflake banged her front hooves on the floor, Ms. Primrose and Sage suddenly froze.

"Snowflake!" squealed Olivia, throwing her arms around her. "You've found your magic!"

"But what magic is it?" said Snowflake, staring

at the icy blue figures of Ms. Primrose and Sage.

"It's freezing magic," Cloud exclaimed. "My mom has it. It means you can freeze people and things for a little while. It doesn't last long, particularly not when you first discover your powers. They'll probably be able to move again any minute!"

"The flames!" said Isabel. "They're going down."

"It's because Ms. Primrose is frozen, so her magic isn't working," explained Cloud. "Now I might be able to help." He stamped his own hooves, and rain clouds appeared again over the whole of the lake. Rain started to fall, and this time the flames fizzled out and died.

There was a cracking noise, and the icy blue started to fade from Ms. Primrose. She slowly started to move. Her face was a mask of horror as she looked around and realized the fire had gone

out. "No!" she shrieked. "What have you done?"

There was the sound of shouts. The magic that had been holding the school doors locked had also faded while Ms. Primrose had been frozen, and the teachers and students were now spilling out of the building, running toward the lake.

"We can't fight them all!" whinnied Sage.

"Gallop!" screamed Ms. Primrose.

"Freeze them!" Olivia urged Snowflake as Sage swung around and began to gallop away.

Snowflake was already stamping her hoof, but although some gold sparks flew up, they were small and weak.

"Snowflake's too exhausted from using the freezing spell," said Cloud.

"We'll catch them!" shouted Sophia, racing after Ms. Primrose on Rainbow. Scarlett and Blaze, Isabel and Cloud, Ava and Star all followed, with Layla and Dancer flying overhead. But the unicorns were tired after all the magic they had done, and Sage seemed to be galloping at twice the usual speed of any unicorn. He disappeared quickly from sight. The girls from Sapphire dorm turned and came back to Olivia and Snowflake.

As they reached them, so did all the students and teachers. Everyone was shouting, wanting to know what had happened.

"Sapphire dorm! What has been going on?" snapped Ms. Nettles.

The girls exchanged looks. "I think it's going to take some time to explain, Ms. Nettles," said Layla.

"Come to my study, then." Ms. Nettles clapped her hands for silence. "The rest of you, I need you to repair all this damage before the parents get here. Please work together using your unicorns' magic. There is to be no arguing. Ms. Rosemary is now in charge!"

In Ms. Nettles's study, the girls explained everything that had been going on.

"I knew Ms. Primrose was up to no good," said Ms. Nettles, shaking her head angrily. "Making locking spells, disappearing for days, giving false information when we were looking for sky berries, and telling Layla not to release the fire beetles into the trees." She rubbed her forehead. "Well done, girls. The lake would have been destroyed without your bravery and courage."

"But why did she do it?" asked Sophia.

Ms. Nettles sighed and shook her head. "Greed for power, I think. She could never be satisfied— and she was terribly jealous of anyone she saw as a threat. When, years ago, I started as a student at Unicorn Academy, I knew I wanted to become head teacher one day. I should have kept that to myself, but foolishly I told Ms. Primrose. From then on she was wary of me. I suspect she guessed that my unicorn, Thyme, would have plant magic, and knowing how I suffer terribly with hay fever, she paired us together. I've often caught her smirking when Thyme is using magic and all I can do is sneeze."

Poor Ms. Nettles! No wonder she was so grumpy. Managing her hay fever with Thyme as her unicorn wouldn't have been easy, Olivia thought.

"So will you become head teacher now?" asked Layla.

Ms. Nettles's thin mouth curved into a smile. "That's for the trustees to decide. But if I'm offered the position, then naturally I will take it." She sneezed and reached for a small brown bottle on her desk. "Excuse me, I think I need some more of my hay fever medicine."

"That's hay fever medicine?" said Ava as Ms. Nettles measured out a capful.

"Yes, without it, I sneeze all the time!"

Sapphire dorm exchanged looks. So Ms. Nettles hadn't been drinking a sinister potion when they'd seen her with a little bottle—it had just been her medicine!

Ms. Nettles glanced at the clock. "There's not much time before the parents arrive, and I must speak to the trustees and tell them what has been happening. Go and get yourselves cleaned up and then get your unicorns ready. You don't want to miss the ball!" She smiled at Olivia. "It looks like all of Sapphire dorm will be graduating, after all!"

Everyone cheered, and Olivia suddenly found herself surrounded by her friends and enveloped in a huge Sapphire dorm hug.

CHAPTER 10

By the time the parents arrived that evening, the academy was looking perfect again. Star and Thyme had regrown the plants and trees, and also grown a path of pink flowers leading from the school to the lake. New decorations hung from the trees, and strands of fairy lights sparkled. Unicorns with food magic had made candy apples and lollipops and hung them from the branches of the trees, and Sherbet, Sam's unicorn, had created a fountain of raspberry lemonade that fizzed and popped as it shot into the air.

Olivia and her friends groomed their unicorns

until they shone, fed them sky berries and lake water to replenish their magic, and then went inside to change into their long sparkly-blue graduation gowns.

Olivia felt a rush of happiness as she looked out their dorm window. "Everywhere looks perfect!"

"I can't believe we'll be leaving here tonight,"

said Layla, seeing the suitcases on their beds, packed and ready to go home with them.

"I'm going to miss you all so much," said Olivia. She glanced around at her friends. "Are you really sure you don't hate me for keeping secrets?"

"Of course we don't hate you!" everyone chorused.

"No more secrets from now on though," said Sophia firmly. "We're a team, and we're so much stronger when we work together."

"We're going to be friends forever," declared Scarlett.

"Friends who keep Unicorn Island safe!" agreed Isabel. "I know we live far away, but we will definitely find ways to meet up. For a start, I don't think we've seen the last of Ms. Primrose."

"If she tries to harm the lake again, we'll stop her!" said Sophia.

"We'll never let her ruin Unicorn Island!" declared Layla.

They all nodded firmly.

"Ooh, look, there's Valentina," said Scarlett, pointing out the window to where Valentina was standing with her parents. She wasn't wearing a graduation gown. "Doesn't she look sulky? It looks like Ms. Nettles has stopped her from graduating."

"Valentina needs to be nicer to Golden Briar before they'll ever bond," piped up Ava. "She never listens to anything Golden Briar has to say."

"I'm very glad I finally listened to Snowflake," said Olivia with a smile.

★

The rest of the afternoon passed in a blur. Parents arrived, students were hugged and kissed, unicorns were patted and stroked. Everyone piled into the gardens and watched as the dorms did their displays. Sapphire dorm had made some last-minute changes to theirs, and the crowd gasped and cheered as Scarlett and Blaze made hoops of fire that Olivia and Snowflake froze as the students and their unicorns jumped through them. Olivia caught sight of her little sister, Matilda, clapping wildly with her parents and felt her heart swell. Matilda was so lucky. After Christmas she would be starting at the academy, making her own friends and having her own adventures.

She's going to have the best time ever, thought Olivia wistfully. Part of her felt sad that she wouldn't be at the academy with her little sister, but seeing Snowflake's parents whinnying proudly as they all bowed at the end of the routine, she knew she wouldn't change a thing!

After the demonstration, all the students who were graduating went into the ballroom. Lit by candles hanging in crystal chandeliers, the room

sparkled prettily. Olivia gave Billy the thumbs-up as she admired the glittering paper swans, eagles, and owls suspended around the room. The boys from Diamond dormitory had done a great job decorating it.

On the stage, at the front, Ms. Nettles gave a speech. Olivia listened carefully, bursting with pride.

"To those of you graduating today, I'm proud of you all. I hope it's a journey you will remember for the rest of your lives. You and your unicorns have now bonded, and I hope you have also made other lifelong friends who will always live in your hearts. Friendship is one of the greatest gifts you can ever give or receive. Whatever you do, wherever you go, make friends, but above all, be a friend." Ms. Nettles paused while the hall erupted with applause. "Now, please come onstage to receive your graduation scrolls."

The students and their unicorns filed onto the stage, and Ms. Nettles and Ms. Rosemary handed out the graduation scrolls, shaking hands with each student in turn as the audience clapped.

"Do we really have to say goodbye?" Olivia whispered to the others as they gathered together. She hadn't thought it was possible to feel so happy and so sad at the same time.

"I guess we do," said Layla.

"It won't be for long," said Ava. "We're going to have lots and lots of sleepovers!"

"Now, girls, no sad faces tonight!" said Ms. Rosemary, coming over to them. Her eyes twinkled. "I know what you're feeling because I felt exactly the same about leaving the academy and my friends when I graduated what feels like a hundred years ago. But I'm sure you'll see each other very often—just like my friends and I do.

And there's always the reunion ball. We hold them so that past students and staff can meet up and share their adventures with our current students."

"That sounds brilliant," exclaimed Scarlett. "Please hold a reunion ball soon, Ms. Rosemary!"

Ms. Rosemary laughed. "Go," she said, shooing the students away with her hands. "It's time to have some fun!"

As they all left the stage, the ball really got going. There were long tables groaning with every kind of food—plates of tiny sandwiches, iced cookies in the shape of unicorns, silver platters piled high with strawberries and cherries, multicolored jellies, ice cream cakes, and sticks of fluffy cotton candy. There was music and dancing in the gardens too. The Sapphire girls had a wonderful time cantering around on their unicorns.

Flushed and happy, Olivia and Snowflake stopped under an apple tree hung with fairy lights. Overhead, stars twinkled and the full moon shone down.

Olivia slipped off Snowflake's back and hugged her. "We did it. We actually graduated."

Snowflake nuzzled her arm. "I always believed we would."

"I just feel so lucky! I've got such amazing friends," said Olivia. "And the best unicorn."

Snowflake's dark eyes met hers. "I'm the lucky one," she said softly. Reaching out, she breathed gently on Olivia's face. "We're going to look after Unicorn Island together forever, Olivia."

Olivia's heart felt like it would burst with happiness. She rested her cheek against Snowflake's blue-and-silver mane, and together they watched the other Sapphire girls dancing with their unicorns. Then, giving her a huge smile, Olivia jumped onto Snowflake's back, and they cantered over to join their best friends under the stars.

PERSONALITY
QUIZ

Which Unicorn Academy
student are YOU most like?
Take this quiz to find out!

On my first day at Unicorn Academy, I . . .

A) Search for magical plants and animals in the grounds
B) Put photos of my family by my bed—I'll miss them!
C) Set up challenges to help my unicorn find their magic straight away!
D) Read everything I can about unicorns in the school library
E) Braid my beautiful unicorn's tail with sparkly ribbons
F) Go for a gallop with my amazing unicorn!

My favorite lesson at Unicorn Academy is . . .

A B C D E F

A) Nature studies
B) Unicorn care
C) None, I just want to be on an adventure!
D) Geography of Unicorn Island
E) Unicorn history
F) Cross-country

My favorite
unicorn
magic is . . .

A) Plant magic
B) Light magic
C) Fire magic
D) Flying magic
E) Ice magic
F) Water magic

I will be a
good guardian of
Unicorn Island
because of
my . . .

A) Creativity
B) Loyalty
C) Bravery
D) Cleverness
E) Kindness
F) Determination

My favorite place to be at Unicorn Academy is . . .

A) In its beautiful gardens
B) Sapphire dormitory, chatting with my friends
C) Exploring the woods
D) Under the reading tree in the library
E) Hanging out with my unicorn in the stables
F) Splashing around in beautiful Sparkle Lake

The READING TREE

Seasonal And Elemental Spells

If you answered. . .

Mostly As

You're Ava, who loves looking after plants and animals with her sweet unicorn, Star.

Mostly Bs

You're Sophia, who is very loyal and who is best friends with her gorgeous unicorn, Rainbow.

Mostly Cs

You're Scarlett, who likes to have fun with her amazing unicorn, Blaze.

Mostly Ds

You're Layla, who adores reading and learning and hanging out with her kind unicorn, Dancer.

Mostly Es

You're Olivia, who is caring and likes to make sure her beautiful unicorn, Snowflake, looks her very best!

Mostly Fs

You're Isabel, who loves to race and is and always up for an adventure with her wonderful unicorn, Cloud.

READ MORE ABOUT

UNICORN ACADEMY

New friends. New adventures.
Find a new series . . . just for you!

ISADORA MOON
For ballerina and fairy and vampire lovers

MAGIC ON THE MAP
For adventurers

UNICORN ACADEMY
For unicorn lovers

PUPPY PIRATES
For dog lovers

PURRMAIDS
For mermaid and cat lovers

BALLPARK Mysteries
For sports fans